REFLECTION OF MOUNT FLAME

CONNOR WHITELEY

No part of this book may be reproduced in any form or by any electronic or mechanical means. Including information storage, and retrieval systems, without written permission from the author except for the use of brief quotations in a book review.

This book is NOT legal, professional, medical, financial or any type of official advice.

Any questions about the book, rights licensing, or to contact the author, please email connorwhiteley@connorwhiteley.net

Copyright © 2023 CONNOR WHITELEY

All rights reserved.

DEDICATION

Thank you to all my readers without you I couldn't do what I love.

CHAPTER 1

Professor Aleshia O'Kin loved Mount Flame.

She didn't know why she loved the amazing mountain that was the tallest in the entire Realm, but there was just something so alluring, amazing and breathtaking about it. It popped up in her dreams, her work, her everything, Aleshia had to find out everything about the mountain.

Even if it killed her.

As Aleshia sat on her favourite wooden rocking chair inside the wonderful log cabin she was staying in, she stared out over the amazing mountain range and towards her obsession, Mount Flame.

Whenever the university asked her why she was requesting funding for yet another expedition to Mount Flame, Aleshia would always give them the same answer, because it was her duty.

In all honesty, she had no idea what that duty was, but if she had ever wondered about leaving the mountain, her research or her field of study (Pre-

Realm History), then that night without fail she would get weird dreams about the Mountain wanting her.

Aleshia tried to push those awful memories away and she simply focused on the amazing view outside the log cabin. The wonderful blankets of thick white snow dusted the entire mountain range, like her favourite sweet sponge cakes she had had as a child.

The wonderful smell of rich bitter coffee with a dash of caramel syrup made Aleshia wrap her hands round her mug of coffee next to her and take a massive sip of the battery acid.

There was something just so peaceful, so wonderful so mysterious about the mountain range that Aleshia had once wondered about living here, just so she could feel the cold bite of the snow every morning, but the university and real life had always called her back.

The sound of people talking, muttering and moving heavy equipment outside made Aleshia frown as that spoiled her perfect silence and she would have sworn she heard the mountains moan in their frustration.

That was probably the only thing Aleshia hated about these expeditions, all these newbies, junior professors and interns that wanted to come along and get famous. She had no idea why they all believed they would get famous just because of they were travelling with an O'Kin.

Aleshia loved exploring the world with her mother, father and brothers as a teenager. She loved discovering ancient cultures, tombs and even some magical weapons, they were fun to use before her father turned them over to the King.

Spoil sport!

But since her parents died and her brothers went off into the military, Aleshia had been left alone, and quite frankly she knew she would never be as great as her parents. They were the true historians, they knew everything about the Realm and all the other races on each side of the borders.

Aleshia hated comparing herself to them, but that was the truth. She felt as if she was playing around, pretending to be far greater than she would ever be normally.

That's why she loved the mountain so much, Aleshia felt like Mount Flame understood her and wanted her to come to it.

And Aleshia wasn't going to disobey.

Then Aleshia stood up and stretched her neck, forcing herself to look away from her beloved mountains, she smiled as she stared at her log cabin with all its desks, files and books scattered around.

Her husband, Charlian O'Kin, just wanted her to clean up, but Aleshia wasn't going to do that. This was her cabin, it was the only space in the Realm where she could work in peace to figure out why Mount Flame wanted, needed her to visit it.

Just the thought of her husband made Aleshia want him here.

After meeting him two decades ago in a lecture

on the unification of the human tribes to form the Realm, Aleshia had travelled everywhere with him, and him her.

They were married on an expedition, they would both stay up late each night talking about their adventures, arguing their hypothesis and celebrating (like married people do) each other's successes.

If Aleshia could have her way, he would be the only person on the expedition, but the university would never allow that sadly.

Aleshia went to take a step forward but her feet touch an opened book, and Aleshia smile's deepened. The opened book was on the very thing that allowed her to get her funding for the expedition.

The Reflection of Mount Flame.

In the tens of thousands of years since Mount Flame's first historical mention only a hundred people had seen this so-called reflection. Aleshia was probably the most recent, and she loved the Mount for it.

It was an impossible thing to describe, but Aleshia always mentioned about how smooth, strange and unnatural Mount Flame looked normally, but sometimes, just sometimes the Mount would become engulfed in fire and the flames would perfectly reflect the sunlight.

When Aleshia first heard it, she knew it was a myth, a lie, a legend but after seeing it and becoming scared out of her wits, Aleshia knew for a fact it was no myth.

But the one thing Aleshia could never understand about the reflection was why only certain people throughout history could see it. When she had witnessed it the first time, she had been standing with her husband, another professor and two interns.

She was the only one who had seen it.

To her amazement, Aleshia's husband hadn't tried to dust her off as a crazy woman, he had tried to help her figure it out and even his dragon had tried to be helpful.

Aleshia wished she could remember her name!

As Aleshia picked up the book, she slowly closed it and wished that the expedition would get underway soon, she had to go to the mountain, she had to see Mount Flame and answer its call.

The entire expedition waited for two things, Charlian to return with his dragon from the university with new equipment after some stupid interns had got drunk and urinated all over it, and most importantly they were all waiting for the weather to clear.

Aleshia hated that factor. From down here the entire mountain range looked so peaceful and wonderful, but if she really focused she could clearly see a thin veil of white around the top of Mount Flame.

Meaning it was a full scale blizzard on the mountain, and no dragon loaded up with crew and equipment could easily survive that.

But Aleshia had to get to Mount Flame, she needed to see it, savour it and answer its divine call.

No matter what others said.
Even her husband.

CHAPTER 2

Honourary Professor Charlian O'Kin leant against the warm stone walls of the university and stared out across the courtyard with its stunning maple trees, roses and talking tomatoes as he waited for the new equipment.

Charlian couldn't deny he didn't love being back at the university in the Capital for the day before he had to fly back off into the frozen wastelands towards Mount Flame.

There was just something good about the university, it felt comforting, alive and filled with knowledge that Charlian just wanted to learn. He loved learning more than anything else in the world (except his wife and dragon, of course) and that was why he became a professor, in a way, because he never ever wanted to stop learning.

The amazing refreshing smell of the roses sent a wave of pleasure down Charlian's spine, the amazing plants at the university was another great benefit.

As the sounds of students talking, laughing and groaning about their latest piece of "impossible" coursework, Charlian just focused on the sense of life here, he was going to miss it when he went to the frozen wastelands.

Charlian loved his wife that was a fact, but he didn't enjoy all the strange locations she wanted to go to. Maybe it was her historical training that made her want to go to these random places, but Charlian wanted to explore the "real" ruins of the past. Like temples, ruins and destroyed cities.

Not some mountain in the middle of nowhere.

Charlian wondered if his military training was partly at fault here. He had always loved to serve as a dragon rider with his dragon, Octon, fighting for the Realm against the orks in the North, the dwarfs in the west and all the damn creatures from the south.

But when he saw that beautiful, sexy Professor Aleshia, he couldn't help but become fascinated by her, her history and her ambitions, and Charlian had learnt a lot of the Realm's history from military school, so he impressed her and the university offered to make him an Honourary Professor.

The sound of massive wings flapping overhead made Charlian excited as he looked up and focused on his amazing dragon float down to the ground. Charlian was always stunned by her beauty with her long wings, deep fiery orange scales and her killer smile.

He was glad he had taught her decades ago how

to hide all her hundreds of dagger-like teeth inside her mouth, because those things were scary.

As Octon landed gently, she smiled and Charlian and he went over to her. Charlian ran his fingers gently over her fiery scales and was amazed by their coldness, he didn't realise how much he had missed waiting for her.

"Got our fish?" Charlian asked.

"Sure thing Boss," Octon said as she waved her massive tail.

Charlian didn't need her to go and catch fish for them whilst he waited, but she had looked like she needed something to do, and Charlian had fond memories of playing in the university's lake when he first met Aleshia, so that seemed the perfect place.

"Professor O'Kin!" a man shouted.

Charlian turned round and frowned when he saw a tall stuck-up looking man wearing a posh black suit walk towards him with a piece of parchment. At least there were ten young men walking behind him carrying boxes of equipment.

"Yes Lord Chancellor Duran," Charlian said. He hated the head of the university.

"I need you to sign these forms saying you will personally cover any costs incurred due to damages on your expedition,"

Charlian laughed. "Why? We didn't need to sign any forms before,"

"That was before you and Professor O'Kin allowed interns to urinate all over the equipment,"

Octon started laughing. Charlian playfully hit her.

"Of course Lord Chancellor," Charlian said bitterly and signed the forms.

Duran turned, clicked his fingers and walked away as the young men came over to Octon and started attaching the boxed of equipment to her.

Charlian looked at Octon. "I don't know why you don't burn him,"

"Cos boss, that's murder. And murder's bad,"

Charlian smiled and shook his head. Aleshia might have called Octon childish, but that was why Charlian loved her. She was a fun, amazing dragon that he would protect to the end, no matter what Aleshia thought.

"True," Charlian said, "how long until we return to the wastelands?"

"Come on boss," Octon said, "it ain't that bad. Mount Flame is fun to fly around, I love rolling about in the snow!"

"So you're prepared for flying to Mount Flame even in a snow storm,"

"Yea!" Octon shouted, "Blizzards are the best!"

"Carrying me, the team and equipment?" Charlian asked.

Octon roared a little and stared at one of the young men as they finished up loading her, Charlian wondered whether or not he had pinched one of her scales.

"My question," Charlian said.

Octon cocked her head. "Does all the team have

to come back?"

Charlian playfully hit her on the nose. "Yes,"

"Then no boss, flying into blizzards isn't fun with other people. Can you and me please fly into one? Pretty please,"

Charlian was probably about to say yes when one of the young men tapped him on the shoulder. He hated that. It was so rude, and why didn't he just call Charlian's name?

Charlian turned. "Yes?"

"You are all loaded up Honourary Professor, and Lord Chancellor Durcan has given you permission to leave," the young men said before walking away.

Charlian and Octon just looked at each other, he had no idea he needed that pompous idiot's permission to leave his place of work. Charlian was now actually looking forward to returning to the frozen wastelands just to get away from Durcan.

But most of all, he was looking forward to seeing the woman he loved once again.

CHAPTER 3

Aleshia loved the amazing bite of the freezing cold wind as it blew across the mountain range towards her. As Aleshia stared out over the thick blanket of crisp white snow that seemed to stretch on for miles upon miles, she couldn't contain her excitement about the expedition edging closer.

The air was crisp, cold and smelt slightly of pine as the wind kept blowing, she was glad it didn't kick up too much of the snow. That would have been horrific as it would have blocked Aleshia's wonderful divine sight of Mount Flame, she had to get there soon.

The mountain was calling her.

As much as Aleshia just wanted to kidnap a dragon and get to Mount Flame as soon as possible, she forced herself to remain rational. She had to wait for her beautiful husband to return with the equipment and Octon.

Aleshia had to smile at the idea of seeing her fit,

sexy husband again and even kissing him on his wonderful soft lips. She was looking forward to that.

In the distance and just above the howling of the wind, Aleshia heard the shouting, talking and moaning of the expedition crew that were probably setting up their own experiments a bit further down in the valley.

It was probably one of the few things she enjoyed about having interns along and even other professors, sometimes they came up with such amazing projects that might have even impressed her parents.

There was one intern that had actually discovered magic crystals in the air once on one of her expeditions using some strange new technology from the Capital. That discovery transformed the Realm's understanding of magic and how it interacted with the natural world, and because of course Aleshia had been expedition leader, she got partial credit.

Aleshia really hoped there would be another breakthrough this time, but she had to get to Mount Flame. It needed her.

Aleshia wore her thickest fur coat, gloves and black fur hat as she started to walk through the snow listening to the crunchy snow under her feet,

As she walked through the snow and tightened her coat around her body, Aleshia saw the interns and other members of the crew putting up tents, installing scientific equipment and some were even having snowball fights.

Aleshia couldn't blame them, but she needed them focused, alert and ready to move out at a moment's notice. Aleshia was about to shout at them when she heard a distinct sound. It sounded like something flapping in the wind then she realised what it was.

She stopped in the snow as massive amounts was kicked up in the air and it was like Aleshia was in a blizzard as something orange and fiery moved in the snowy conditions.

When the snow settled, Aleshia smiled at the massive fiery orange dragon that stood in front of her. Aleshia heard the interns start to rush over to unload the equipment, but all she could do was stare at the majesty and utter beauty of the dragon.

Octon looked as if she was a child of Mount Flame with her stunning colours and divine ability to roar out fire, Aleshia shook her head as she needed to remain calm, logical and rational. Mount Flame was something to be studied, not something to fall in love with.

Then the most beautiful man Aleshia had ever seen slid off the dragon and walked towards her, Aleshia could only stare with a smile that went across her entire face at the man she loved.

Aleshia couldn't believe how even in these icy frozen conditions, her palms were turning sweaty and her heart skipped a few beats as she stared at Charlian's tight black coat, long brown hair and amazing smile that could probably melt the entire mountain range if he really tried.

And in that moment, Aleshia didn't even care if he melted or damaged Mount Flame. She was so pleased to see him.

When Charlian wrapped his strong arms around her, Aleshia was in heaven and she pressed her lips against his wonderful warm soft lips that she would happily kiss all day.

"Professor?" a man asked and completely ruined the mood.

Aleshia sadly broke the kiss and turned to face the little short man who dared to talk to her. She hated the man's grey fur coat, cheesy grin and dark brown eyes, he just looked silly.

"Professor," the man said, "I was wondering where you want us to store the equipment for the flight,"

Aleshia really focused on the man now as she realised he was talking to the Lead Intern Harriton, the person who looked after them when Aleshia was busy with other things. She still didn't want to talk to him, she wanted to be with her husband, but she was a leader first.

"Keep them here for now please. We will investigate the weather conditions on the mount top then we launch if appropriate," Aleshia forced herself to say.

She didn't want to launch if it was appropriate, she wanted to launch immediately no matter what the weather conditions were like. She was going to Mount

Flame whether people liked it or not.

Aleshia looked at her husband. "I missed you,"

Octon walked forward. "I missed ya too girly. Want did I miss? Any fights?"

Aleshia and Charlian just looked at each other, and Aleshia truly knew that their strange little family was back together, and at least one of the two things they were waiting for had come together.

Now she just needed the weather conditions to make it safe to fly up there, but Aleshia would have sworn she had heard something being carried in the wind.

She turned to look at Mount Flame and she couldn't see it. Aleshia's felt her stomach twist, tighten and churn as she feared something terrible had happened to her mountain.

Then the entire mountain range shone like hundreds of fireworks had been shot up in the air.

Mount Flame was shining bright. It was reflecting every little piece of light it could at her.

Aleshia smile and her mouth dropped.

"What ya looking at?" Octon asked.

"Mount Flame," Aleshia said, "It's so beautiful,"

Her husband placed a loving hand on her shoulder. "Babe, I don't see anything,"

CHAPTER 4

Charlian was gutted that he couldn't see the reflection of Mount Flame, he really, really wanted to. He wanted to be able to talk about its so-called beauty and stunning appearance with his wife, but that clearly wasn't going to happen.

And in all honesty, Charlian didn't really care too much. He was perfectly content with the stunning beauty of his amazing wife that he only wanted to kiss, hug and do more adult things with after not seeing her for so long.

But as she was so engrossed in the reflection of Mount Flame, Charlian had to admit he still hated the mountain range. It really was such an awful frozen wasteland as far as he was concerned, it was freezing cold and there was nothing obvious here to study.

As harsh as it sounded they were only there because of his wife's obsessions with Mount Flame, and part of the entire reason he had agreed to come here was because he just wanted her to get it all over and done with.

He hoped as soon as she had finished with Mount Flame, they could return to the Capital and study real Pre-realm history and put all this stuff about the mountain behind them.

He just wanted his wife back, was that so wrong?

Charlian felt the wonderfully warm snout of Octon snuggle into his neck as they watched Aleshia do her thing, but after a few minutes Charlian realised she wasn't going to be moving any time soon, so he had to do something.

"Babe?" Charlian asked.

Aleshia was standing there perfectly still as if Mount Flame had her in some kind of hypnotic trance that she wasn't strong enough to break, Charlian tapped her on the shoulder and even the Lead Intern Harriton tapped her.

Aleshia frowned and must have forced herself to look away. "What!"

Charlian took a step back. "I was wondering if you were okay. You were acting strange,"

"I was fine. I was just studying the reflection. If you were a real professor you would know that!" Aleshia shouted.

Charlian heard Octon snarl a little and he kissed her snout and focused on his wife.

"I'm..." Aleshia said softly, "I'm sorry. I'm under a lot of stress. I just want this expedition to go well. I need to prove I'm as great as my parents,"

Charlian took a step forward and held Aleshia's

gloved hands. "You will always be amazing to me,"

She smiled and looked at Octon. "Want to fly up there?"

Octon smiled. "Course Alesh. I wanna smash into some mountains, roar in a blizzard and fly into a storm,"

Charlian coughed.

"But seriously girly? Boss says that a bad idea with living people on it,"

Aleshia let go of Charlian's hands. "We know he's boring,"

As Aleshia kept talking with Octon, he started to feel his stomach tighten as she wasn't acting like the woman she normally was. The Aleshia he knew, loved and had married was always safety obsessed, careful and methodological.

She never would have talked about flying up in a blizzard normally. Something was very, very wrong.

"Na girly. If you wanna fly into a blizzard, you need another dragon. I valuable boss's opinions,"

Charlian stared at his wife. "What's up with you today?"

Aleshia threw her arms up in the air. "What's wrong with me! I am the only person trying to keep this expedition together!"

Charlian was about to say something back when he saw all the Interns and other members of the expeditionary team was watching him, Octon and Aleshia.

He had been on enough expeditions to know the

costs of the crew not seeing the leader as strong and capable. Charlian had to help Aleshia but he couldn't have the crew lose faith in her either.

And now Charlian couldn't shake the feeling that something a lot darker was going on now.

"Professor Aleshia," Charlian said calmly. Then Aleshia focused and looked around and smiled.

"Yes Charlian, we will start to investigate the weather conditions. I estimate the Mount should be clear in the next few hours for the mission to go ahead,"

As calm as his wife seemed now, Charlian knew that the crew were still suspicious as they exchanged glances with each other, and Charlian knew why instantly. The blizzard was starting to get heavier and heavier.

Even Charlian was now ankle deep in snow, they couldn't go to the mountain top today.

And the thought of telling his wife that scared him more than he wanted to admit.

CHAPTER 5

Aleshia hated this blizzard, Charlian and his dumb dragon Octon. The entire crew was just plain stupid too, how dare they all try to stop her from seeing, studying and worshipping her divine Mount Flame.

It wasn't her fault that they were all too weak, pathetic and ugly to see the divinity of the Mount. It was her divine birthright that she had been allowed to see the reflection of the mountain in all its stunning majesty.

As Aleshia stared out of the window of her log cabin, she couldn't help but focus on Mount Flame and the stunning reds, oranges and yellows that engulfed the mountain like it was actually on fire. She could almost hear the loud immense crackling of the Mountain as if it was a real fire.

Then as the sun started to set, Aleshia's mouth dropped open as the reflection started to look even more impressive in the darkening sky. She had to get there, she had to study the mountain, she had to learn why it had chosen her and not the others.

Aleshia might not have cared why it didn't choose them, but that was the excuse she needed to continue lying about, she had to keep them on her side. She couldn't afford for the idiots on the crew to make them all leave her, and she most certainly couldn't allow her husband to leave her.

Aleshia had watched him outside before the blizzard had apparently gotten dangerous, he doubted her and what if he was now conspiring with her enemies at the university to steal her grand discovery away from her.

Yes that had to be it. Her husband had betrayed all of his wedding vows and she was going to make him pay, even if it was the last thing she ever did.

As two massive stunning arms wrapped around her, Aleshia pushed all those silly ideas out of her mind as she realised they weren't true, and Aleshia breathed in the heavenly scent of her husband. Even in these amazing mountains he still smelt great.

Aleshia forced herself away from the mountain and just stared into those wonderful warm caring eyes, and she just wanted to enjoy him for a few moments before she had to focus back on the mountain.

A tiny part of her wondered why she couldn't just leave Mount Flame and just run away with Charlian, they had spoken about it more than enough times, and they had even considered joining the

Military Historical Society and helping the military explore the land to the south of the Realm where all the trolls, goblins and other creatures lived.

But as much as Aleshia loved the idea of the adventure, action and learning that could give her, she had to focus on Mount Flame. It had chosen her, loved her and wanted her, even in the wonderfully strong arms of her husband, she still felt as if the mountain could give her something more, that her husband never ever could.

"What is up with you today?" Charlian asked.

Aleshia took a few deep breaths of the cold coffee-scented air as she reminded herself that he only loved her and wanted the best for her, her expedition and her reputation.

"You know what honey. I just… I just wanted this to be a success,"

"And it will,"

Aleshia wrapped her own arms around him. "But what if it isn't? What if the crew dessert me?"

"They won't. We pay them enough. I wouldn't let anything happen to you,"

As their lips met, Aleshia suppressed her smile as that was exactly the answer she had wanted, she wanted her husband to be loyal to the divine Mount Flame, she wouldn't tolerate any disobedience against the mountain's wishes, and all of them had to go on the trip no matter what.

She just had to convince her husband to support her.

Aleshia didn't know why she needed everyone to go to the mountain, but she just knew that that was what Mount Flame wanted, and obviously the mountain knew best.

"How many peeps can Octon take?" Aleshia asked.

Charlian broke the kissing and cocked his head. "I thought only you, me and three interns were going up,"

Aleshia shrugged. "Yea, but this is a once in a lifetime opportunity. Shouldn't everyone get to see it?"

"I suppose so and," he said, "I suppose if everyone went then it would give us more bodies to study Mount Flame,"

Aleshia gave him a devilish smile, she had trained him well and now she finally knew what argument to use to continue convincing him.

"That's a good point honey," Aleshia said, "especially if your theory is true about there being some kind of device in the mountain,"

Aleshia still hated that theory of Charlian, to think that the glory of Mount Flame wasn't magical, natural and just created by some piece of ancient technology was heresy to her.

Mount Flame was glorious without any need of some technology to improve it.

Charlian nodded.

"We have a crew of thirty people," Aleshia said. "How many trips is that on Octon?"

"She isn't a carriage or taxi. She is a living breathing dragon," Charlian said firmly.

Aleshia almost rolled her eyes, him and that damn dragon. She didn't need a dragon right now, Aleshia needed a slave to work for her and force them to do as they were told.

"Of course honey. I'm really sorry," Aleshia said kissing with again. "How many trips? I don't want it to be too many or she might get too tired,"

It was all lies and Aleshia loved lying to her husband now, it was fun, exciting and she had never felt so alive before now. She was even starting to wonder what having an affair was like.

"About five trips should be enough,"

Aleshia gave Charlian a seductive smile and pulled him close. He had answered her very well, and now she was going to reward him for his good behaviour, and by the time the morning came, she just knew the blizzard would be gone and the true mission could begin.

And Aleshia could finally serve Mount Flame like it had always wanted her to.

CHAPTER 6

Charlian didn't want to believe his stunning wife was going crazy, being corrupted by something or simply becoming possessed by the mountain, but at this point he really didn't know what to believe.

As Charlian stepped outside and looked over the horrible frozen wastelands with the sun rising over the unnaturally smooth cone-shape of Mount Flame, he couldn't help but feel his skin crawl.

He didn't want to be here. He didn't want anyone to be here, but he had to find out what was going on.

He hadn't been that surprised when his wife had tried to convince him to take all those people up into the mountain, it was clear she was going crazy but now Charlian was torn between helping her and stopping her.

As Aleshia's husband, he didn't want to challenge her because he could easily be the one that was going crazy, but deep, deep down he knew that he was right and it was Aleshia that was becoming a danger to herself, him and the entire expeditionary team.

Charlian hadn't served in the military for two decades protecting the humans and the Realm just for his wife to start killing innocent people in the name of Mount Flame.

Charlian could hear shouting, barking orders and other softer sounds in the distance and to his surprise he recognised those shouts were coming from Aleshia. That made no sense at all, he had been with his amazing wife for more years than he cared to remember and she never got angry on an expedition.

She was always the wonderful, calm and caring one, this wasn't like her.

Charlian shut the log cabin door behind him and wanted to go over to where the shouting was coming from, but Octon walked (stomped more like) round the log cabin and settled herself right in front of him.

Even in the dim morning light, she still looked beautiful with the amazing light perfectly bouncing off her fiery orange scales.

"What ya girl moaning about?" Octon asked.

"I don't know," Charlian said, "but do the dragons have any myths, legends or rumours about Mount Flame?"

"Oo yes boss," Octon said with a massive grin, "our most famous myth is the Mount is the resting place of the first-ever human to ride a dragon,"

Charlian smiled and shook his head. Sure the Realm had a similar history story for this region because before the Dragon Riders and the Treaty of Fire, which stopped all fighting between the humans, dragons and elves, riding a dragon was thought of as impossible.

Yet someone had managed it, lived their life fighting for truth, justice and fairness before dying on the field of battle to save what would now be considered the Realm.

Charlian had no idea that person was buried here.

"But if that's true then why would the Mount be calling Aleshia?" Charlian asked.

"I donno boss. The rumours only say that the human beat the dragon every night and when the dragon laid its rider to rest in a cave in the Mount…"

Charlian cocked his head and his eyes narrowed on Octon. "What?"

"Well boss, ta dragon laid him to rest and unleashed all its fire. Killing itself in the process and engulfing the mountain in enteral flame to make sure the dragon rider stayed dead forever,"

Charlian just stared at Octon in silence. There was nothing he could say to that, and even in his military days he had been fought plenty of magical enemies but the idea that something would engulf a mountain in flames forever.

It sounded so strange and ridiculous, but a part of him feared what that was what his wife was seeing.

"I heard that myth too," Aleshia said from behind Octon.

When Octon stomped away and settled firmly

behind him, Charlian smiled at his beautiful stunning wife with her fit body, beautiful face and her long sexy hair. She wasn't happy but at least there were all thirty of the crew behind her.

But the more he focused on the crew wearing their thick fur coats, the more Charlian started to realise they didn't look okay. They even looked a bit obsessed like Aleshia.

"What going on girly?" Octon asked.

"I have told the crew the truth. You are hiding the real reason for our expedition, you wanted to hide the fact that there are thousands of coins and gold bars and jewels up on the mountain top," Aleshia said calmly.

Charlian even saw some of the crew spat at his feet. He didn't want what his wife was playing at, she clearly wanted the crew not to trust him, he just didn't know why. Was she really that paranoid that she thought he would plot against her?

Charlian really wasn't liking this one bit. At least the weather had cleaned up so hopefully they would all start to fly there.

Charlian decided to play along. "Of course, I'm sorry everyone. I just didn't want us to get distracted with the riches. We are here for historical value first, then fame then riches,"

Everyone nodded to that. But judging by Aleshia's face, she wasn't impressed.

"Professor Charlian," Harriton said stepping forward.

"Yes," Aleshia said jumping in before Charlian could.

Harriton didn't look sure, but Charlian nodded.

"All interns and crew are ready for deployment. We can fly the moment *you* are ready Professor Charlian,"

Charlian smiled and mouthed *thank you* to him, he didn't know how many his wife was convincing, but things were clearly turning desperate and he needed to get as many allies as possible in case Aleshia really started to turn crazy.

"Thank you," Aleshia said, "everyone will leave here in five minutes. Glory awaits us!"

As soon as she said that, Aleshia walked away and Charlian clicked his fingers and Octon came extremely close to his mouth.

"What's wrong boss?"

"I once heard that dragons can mind talk with people. Please tell me you can do that?" Charlian asked very quietly.

Octon rose on and swung her head gently from side to side. It was almost like she was actually considering it.

+Can do boss. Just donno know how good it is.+ Octon said into Charlian's mind.

+Perfect+

+Why did ya wanna talk like this+

+Because I want you to watch my wife carefully. She isn't right. I think the mountain might be corrupting her+

Octon gave Charlian a little kiss on the head and smiled.

+Don't worry boss I'll protect ya. And I'll even kill her for ya if needed+

As much as Charlian wanted to say that wouldn't be needed, he couldn't be sure.

But if it was. Charlian had to make sure he was the one that killed his wife.

CHAPTER 7

Aleshia couldn't believe how pathetic her husband was, he wasn't the man she had married. Charlian use to be an amazing, strong man who would never ever allow anyone to push him over, but clearly that man was dead.

She couldn't even believe she had put him over the glorious sexy Mount Flame yesterday. The Mountain was divine, it was beautiful and so strong, not like her pathetic wet husband who couldn't even admit she was lying to the crew.

As Aleshia, the crew and her pathetic husband started to load up Octon with all the nets of equipment, she forced herself not to react to the disgusting people here. It was stupid that Aleshia had ever liked any of them, these mortals were so weak compared to Mount Flame, and Aleshia had been chosen by the divine spirits of the mountain unlike these plebs.

As the crew and her husband loaded up the last

of the equipment, Aleshia loved smelling their fearful sweat in the air and listening their feet crunch on the wonderfully thick snow. That snow was a gift from Mount Flame and like all the mountain's gifts, Aleshia had to serve, love and obey it.

And right now Mount Flame wanted them all to get a move on, it wanted her to come to it and bring all these delicious sacrifices. Aleshia had to agree with her divine Mount Flame that all these people would make the most delicious sacrifices and-

Charlian rubbed her shoulders slightly and kissed her on the neck, Aleshia loved that amazing feeling. She loved her husband and everyone on the crew, she couldn't let anything happen to them.

Especially as she was expedition leader, she had to keep everyone safe, and as much as something inside her kept telling her to run away from Mount Flame. Aleshia's curiosity was growing each second about the secrets of the mountain.

"Already Professors," Harriton said.

Charlian extended out his hand to Aleshia and she took it as he helped her climb up onto Octon and Charlian wrapped his strong arms around her.

Aleshia loved it how he was going to protect her no matter what, but she wasn't a fan of the hard leather saddle that she sat on. It felt hard, rough and extremely uncomfortable.

Then four other interns climbed inside the nets carrying the equipment. As dangerous and deadly as it looked, Aleshia knew from countless times of flying by dragon that it was perfectly safe.

And a damn bit more comfortable than sitting on a leather dragon saddle. At least she had the amazing feelings of Charlian's strong arms around her.

"Ready?" Charlian said in her ear.

Aleshia blew out a thick column of vapour that froze instantly in the conditions and even her fingers were starting to feel numb, but she was ready.

She nodded. "Of course. And everyone else be prepared to climb on and join us the moment Octon returns for you all. We're all going to enjoy this trip. Glory awaits us!"

"Glory awaits us!" everyone shouted.

As Charlian spoke to Octon about the trip and taking off, Aleshia heard a strange whooshing sound in the back of her mind and when she looked at Mount Flame it was engulfed in bright black flames.

Aleshia felt something shiver and slip over her skin that made her feel amazing. This was going to be an amazing trip and she had been the divine Chosen One that would free her master from his resting place, so he could walk free amongst men once again.

Aleshia laughed when Octon gently flapped her massive fiery orange wings and they were floating in the air. Then Octon slowly started to flap more and more and they were off.

Aleshia loved the feeling of the fast-moving wind over her skin as they flew. The entire mountain range looked so small from up here.

The deafening howl of the wind was immense

and she loved it. It was amazing. This must have been what the glorious Mount Flame experienced every day.

Octon started to fly straight towards Mount Flame.

Aleshia knew no one else could see it but Mount Flame was so beautiful with its massive black flames.

Even the howl of the wind was dead now. Being replaced completely with the amazing symphony of flame crackling and the people screaming as the flames engulfed them.

It was so beautiful.

Wind shot past.

Octon shook.

The nets shook.

One snapped away.

Equipment flew down.

Someone screamed.

Another gust hit them.

Then another.

Then another.

Mount Flame was testing them.

It was glorious.

Charlian told everyone to hold on.

He wrapped his arms around her.

Aleshia smiled.

More gusts hit them.

Octon shot into the air.

Spinning around.

Gusts hit them from all directions.

Octon froze.
Plunging towards the ground.
Everyone screamed.
They were going to die.

CHAPTER 8

Charlian flat out hated Mount Flame. First it wanted them there. Now it tried to kill them with these awful gusts of wind. It was just ridiculous!

Octon kept dropping.

Charlian felt his stomach lift up.

He could see the ground more and more.

He gripped Aleshia tight.

She didn't seem to care. She wanted this. Damn her!

Charlian didn't want to die. He had to protect everyone. He had to save his wife.

He kicked Octon. Hard.

She shook free.

She flapped her wings.

More gusts hit them.

Charlian was almost thrown off.

Another gust hit.

Aleshia flew to one side.

Charlian almost lost her.

Aleshia screamed. She was smiling. She loved this.

Octon flew harder and harder.

She zoomed towards Mount Flame.

The gusts got more intense.

Charlian held on tight.

The snow lashed down at them.

Hail started.

Pounding into Charlian's head.

Pain flooded his body.

Octon hissed.

She roared.

Her wings slowed.

She was getting tired. She was failing. She was going down again.

"If I die. I cannot come to you," Aleshia said into the wind.

Then everything went silent and perfectly still as all the snow, hail and wind disappeared revealing a stunning beautiful day out on the mountain range.

As Octon kept on flying towards the perfectly smooth coned-shaped Mount Flame, Charlian couldn't help but feel his stomach tighten into a knot at what had just happened.

It was clear the mountain had tried to kill them, but it had obeyed Aleshia. That wasn't normal, right or fair. Maybe the mountain only wanted her alive, maybe the mountain just wanted to kill them all no matter what.

Charlian had to do something but he was out of

options. His head was still spinning from the idea that Mount Flame was alive somehow and could attack them whenever it wanted.

Charlian gently started to stroke Octon as he forced his mind to send his thoughts to her.

+That wasn't natural was it?+ Charlian send.

+Na boss. That ain't no storm. It was magic+

Charlian shook his head at that. He had encountered plenty of witches, warlocks and wizards in his military days and not all of them were good. He couldn't understand how a mountain could become magical even to be able to attack at will.

But he'd be lying if he said his wife didn't bother him more than anything else.

+Do you know where the magic came from?+ Charlian asked, wanting to be wrong.

+Come on boss, ya know it came from tha mountain,"

Charlian nodded. He didn't want that answer but it was clearly the only one that was going to make sense.

+Orders boss man?+

+Fly us to the mountain as before and be careful+

Octon just nodded and soared up high into the sky, and Charlian just smiled as everything below them became so small and not a single cloud was in the sky. It was a perfectly warm cloudless day in the frozen wastelands.

He didn't like that, Charlian knew it wasn't

natural so something else had to be going on. He just hoped he could stop it in time.

When Charlian heard Aleshia gasp, he looked slightly ahead and his mouth dropped at the stunning site of Mount Flame. It was even more impressive up close than it had been on the ground.

The entire mountain was perfectly smooth and in a perfect cone-shape that seemed to defy all laws of nature, the entire place wasn't natural!

And the closer they got to Mount Flame, the more pine, chocolate and coffee Charlian could smell in the air, that alone was strange but after everything that had just happened, the strange smell didn't even make the top ten.

"Circle the top a couple of times," Charlian said coldly and felt Aleshia huff.

Octon nodded and started to circle. Charlian wanted to check out the top first before they landed just to make sure it was solid rock and not soft ice.

From what Charlian could see, the top of Mount Flame was perfectly smooth black granite that reflected the sunlight perfectly for some reason. He wanted to imagine that this was the cause for their expedition and they could now leave.

But he doubted it.

Even the shiny black granite didn't explain the historical and Aleshia's claims about the flames that engulfed Mount Flame, something else had to be causing it.

"Land!" Aleshia shouted.

+Do it please+ Charlian send.

Slowly Octon started their descent and as the perfectly smooth granite got closer and closer Charlian started to feel his skin crawl as something unnatural was clearly here.

When Octon landed with a gentle thud, Charlian could sense his beautiful dragon was disturbed and clearly didn't want to be here either, Charlian didn't know if he would make Aleshia and the two surviving interns turn back now.

But he was still an honourary professor and he had to find out the historical value of the mountain, no matter what.

The mountain top was easily the size of five football pitches and had never received any major damage, but Charlian doubted Mount Flame would ever allow itself to be attacked or damaged.

The air smelt even stronger of coffee, chocolate and pine now and it only seemed to be growing stronger and stronger with each passing second.

Charlian bend down and ran his fingers over the toasty warm granite, even that was a tat strange. The mountain range was still a frozen wasteland at the end of the day, so even the heat from the sun wouldn't be able to heat up the black granite this good.

It was almost like there was a heat source under the surface, like in the mountain itself.

A tiny part of him wondered if it was the dragon that the legend said engulfed the mountain in Pre-Realm history, but that idea only scared him.

Whatever was going on wasn't good, natural or divine.

It was evil.

And that terrified Charlian more than he wanted to admit.

CHAPTER 9

Aleshia loved the amazing top of Mount Flame more than anything else in the entire world. The smooth sexy black granite was so wonderful to run her fingers across, it was like the mountain itself was pulsing its love up her arm and into her heart.

She almost wanted to orgasm at the amazing pleasure it was sending into it, and now she was here Aleshia had, just had to start serving her Master's divine will, because he needed her.

Aleshia had no idea why she felt this strong urge to serve something, she used to think of herself as a strong capable person, but now that she was up here on the top of Mount Flame, she could feel all her will disappearing.

And she loved it!

Even the divine smells of the coffee, chocolate and pine were an instant boost to her energy levels, it had to be Mount Flame wanting her to feel loved and comfortable here.

Aleshia wondered if her pathetic husband thought of this place as a death trap or creepy, but she didn't care. He was just another idiot or who had not been chosen by the divine mountain.

She had been and she was going to honour every single wish of the mountain, no matter what it cost her.

As the sound of Octon's wings flapping grew louder and louder, Aleshia felt more excitement build as the dragon flew off again to get more sacrifices… interns to come up here and help out.

Aleshia had wondered about unloading the equipment here before Octon went off on her second of five trips, but Aleshia needed people to get into the nets so more people could be transported at a time.

Aleshia felt her pathetic husband's hand on her shoulder and she instantly realised how bad their marriage had been. She had never loved him, but the mountain did, and compare to Mount Flame her weak husband would always lose.

"I unloaded one net for us to get started," Charlian said as he pointed behind Aleshia.

"Good thank you," Aleshia said, fighting to keep her rage in check. He had just stopped her from getting more crew to the mountain top.

He was definitely plotting against her. She willed Mount Flame to help her get rid of him.

Aleshia and Charlian went over to the equipment that the two interns were laying out, and Aleshia was hardly impressed. The only equipment on the ground was a few crates of food, drink and some primitive climbing gear.

None of the climbing gear would be good enough until the stronger ropes came. Sure there were some harnesses and even some sword-proof rope, but until the pulleys came up along with some other things, the expedition was yet again at a standstill.

No doubt thanks to her pathetic husband. He was actively and obviously trying to stop her!

"Did you want a snack?" Charlian asked in a disgustingly smooth suggestive tone.

Aleshia understood that he loved her, but she never loved him, and how dare he try to be nice to her now.

Aleshia went close to his ear. "You're aren't going to stop me. I will find the Mas… man in the mountain,"

Charlian's eyes narrowed. "What man?"

Aleshia just laughed. This was the true extent of his ignorance and weakness, if the mountain had even dared to show him a fraction of its power then his poor little mind would probably break.

Then Aleshia realised that she was truly so much grander than her parents and brothers ever had been or would be, sure they might have been famous historians that were behind some of the most important finds in history.

But it was Aleshia who was the truly grand person. She was so great that even Mount Flame (a mystery tens of thousands of years old) had chosen her of all people to see its secrets.

That was how great she was.

"The man that tells me the secrets. The man that will make be famous. The man who will raise… help me raise up in the history books,"

Aleshia wanted to just laugh again at her husband but under her feet, she could have sworn that something was moving and in the very back of her mind… Aleshia wondered if something was leaking in there, like someone had a back door to her mind.

Allowing her to access all this information that only the divine Mount Flame had.

"Babe, I'm worried about you," Charlian asked.

"Pathetic you really are," Aleshia said frowning. "Do you think the mountain cares about your worries? No it only cares about me and revealing its secrets!"

Charlian took a step back and even the two surviving interns looked a bit confused at Aleshia. Their eyes looked so fearful, so scared, so weak.

Aleshia wanted to lick her lips at them but she forced away the gesture. That honour was for the mountain only.

And she was never going to allow herself to put her own benefits and desires over the mountain.

The entire mountain shook.

The granite cracked.

Then Aleshia's face lit up as she watched the smooth black granite melt away in the very middle to reveal a staircase down into the mountain.

They didn't need some strange stupid climbing equipment for Mount Flame protects!

And she was going to protect the mountain in return.

CHAPTER 10

As Charlian forced himself to go over to the massive staircase made from shiny black granite, he felt his stomach painfully tighten. None of this was natural in the slightest and he knew the longer he stayed here, the worse this expedition could go.

He wanted to leave never to return and leave his once-beautiful wife forever, but now Charlian couldn't shake the feeling that she was nothing short of pure evil.

And if his military service had taught him anything, it was that evil had to be stopped no matter what.

Where Charlian's mission had once been about exploring, history and discovery with his wife. It was now about finding out what Mount Flame truly was and stopping the evil within regardless of his own safety.

Charlian's eyes narrowed on the disgraceful granite staircase that leant down into the mountain, so deep that Charlian couldn't see the bottom. The hairs on the back of his neck were starting to stand up, and Charlian could even hear the heavy breathing of the two interns behind him.

He hated heavy breathing!

"Come on pathetic husband!" Aleshia shouted as she started to walk down the stairs.

Charlian froze. Something really wasn't right here, this was far, far, far from the woman he married, loved and wanted to spend the rest of his life with. She was a completely different woman, and Charlian had to find out how to save or kill her.

Charlian looked at the two skinny interns and they both shrugged.

"Stay up here and warn Octon not to bring any more people up here," Charlian said calmly.

He didn't want anyone else to die or become in danger, Charlian wanted to protect life, not damn it.

+In take you can hear me, I love you and I need your help+ Charlian sent to Octon, hoping that she could hear him despite the distance between them.

Charlian turned back to the staircase and took a few deep breaths of the coffee, pine and chocolate scented air. He didn't want to go down there, but this was his duty.

"Come on Mr Pathetic-O'kin," Aleshia said.

Charlian frowned and took his first step down into Mount Flame. But even the stairs felt strange, from granite he was expecting something hard, unbreakable and uncomfortable.

Yet as Charlian took more and more steps down into the mountain, the more spongier the stairs got, they didn't feel like they were made from granite. They felt more like a new technology called memory foam, at least that what was Charlian had read in some new journal at the university.

Then slowly the sunlight coming in from the entrance at the top of Mount Flame got dimmer and dimmer and dimmer.

Charlian spun around.

The top was sealing back up.

Charlian ran back up.

Screaming filled the air.

And as Charlian stood there in the pitch black as the last of the granite regrew to cover up the opening, he knew that the two interns he had wanted to protect were now dead.

Charlian placed his hands on the regrown granite and it was almost burning hot, clearly all that remained of those interns were now charred husks of nothing.

His stomach tightened even more painfully now and Charlian really wanted to escape from here, but he had to find out the reason for all of this, and if there was a larger threat to the Realm.

"I cannot come to you without him!" Charlian heard Aleshia shout into the staircase.

It was moments like that that made Charlian wonder if she was really gone, or maybe the woman he married managed to regain control for short periods of time in-between Mount Flame's corrupting influence.

Then tiny lines of fire spread along the smooth black granite walls of the staircase and Charlian could once again see perfectly. He could see every little detail of each granite step and Charlian got the feeling that the mountain really wanted him to start hurrying up.

Charlian nodded, as if in some kind of gesture of respect to the mountain, and then he started to walk down the stairs again, quicker than last time.

Charlian wasn't going to risk the mountain turning its fury on him, so he hurried and hurried and hurried.

After a few minutes of quickly walking down the steps, he started to see the bottom of the staircase and his wife.

But Charlian almost second guessed himself, Aleshia didn't look like herself for a moment. Each time Charlian blinked, her form flickered from the beautiful woman he married to something else.

Charlian had no idea how to describe it but it was horrific. Aleshia's hair was long jet black with barred wire lovingly twisted into it, and her face was scarred and there was something dark in her eyes, like she was possessed.

Despite his years of experience telling him people couldn't be demonically possessed in one blink then not in the other, Charlian was really starting to doubt how much he knew about the world.

When he reached the bottom of the staircase, Charlian's eyes narrowed on the box-like chamber they were in. The chamber was easily three metres by three metres, but the strange part was everything looked to be made out of volcanic rock.

That was beyond strange for the region because all Charlian's and Aleshia's research showed that none of these mountains were made by volcanic eruptions. The chamber he was in said differently.

Charlian focused on each of the little fiery lines that illuminated the chamber for him and that's when he noticed how strange the lines themselves were.

When Charlian really focused on a particular line, he saw hundreds, maybe thousands of screaming faces in-between each of the flames.

He even thought he saw the faces of the two interns who had died only moments ago.

"Beautiful isn't it?" Aleshia asked.

"You aren't my wife," Charlian said coldly, "Who the hell are you?"

Aleshia coughed a few times and pointed to a massive stone wall that Charlian had completely missed. The wall was nothing special but it didn't have any little lines of fire, and it was covered in little symbols and carvings of some kind of animal.

Charlian didn't know what kind. The creature in question looked to be a mixture of lion, dragon and human. Nothing in the history books even came close to describing such a creature.

Aleshia touched the door and smiled. "I am

home again my love. Let me in,"

Charlian wished he had had time to get a knife or something, because he really had the urge to stab whoever his woman was now. There was no way his wife would have known about touching the door, Charlian had to act.

But he had nothing to act on.

The door melted away.

Aleshia ran off inside.

Charlian followed her.

He had to see this through.

CHAPTER 11

As a professor of Pre-Realm history, Aleshia stared in wonder at the amazing volcanic rock cave they were in. It was stunning how the massive cave had rough walls and the little lines of fire lit it up perfectly.

There was nowhere else she would rather be, it was just breathtaking and there was even something shimmering over on the other side of the cave.

Aleshia didn't hesitate as she started to walk over to it, she was a little surprised at how hot it was in the cave. She could feel tiny drops of sweat start to roll down her back, and considering she was inside a mountain that was inside a frozen mountain range. That was strange.

But as the glorious chosen of Mount Flame, this was heaven and her chance to prove herself for her rightful accession into the true heavens where she could see Mount Flame and be rewarded for her courage.

If the mountain had chosen anyone else, then it would be gravely disappointed, but Aleshia was mighty, grand and powerful unlike her pathetic husband so it was only right she was here.

She was more than glad Mount Flame had taken its sacrifices in the form of those two pointless mortal interns. They were clearly unworthy and now Aleshia had to kill her weak useless husband when the time was right.

A wave of discomfort raised up within her at that idea, but she quickly forced it back down. She didn't need any of those weak human emotions.

She only needed the mountain.

As Aleshia went over to the shimmering object on the other side of the cave, she heard the awful breathing of Charlian. She wished he would just stop breathing and fall down dead.

She pinched herself.

That idea was flat out wrong of her, it was never up to her when these people died. That divine honour was up to the mountain and the mountain alone.

Aleshia bit her tongue hard to punish herself for those disgraceful thoughts.

When she reached the other side of the cave, Aleshia's eyes lit up in happiness as she saw the most amazing thing ever. She stared at a solid square mass of something covered in a thick layer of ash.

The more she stared at the solid mass of something, the more she felt like this was her ultimate desire. If she touched, freed and served whatever was inside then all her wildest dreams could and would come true.

She needed to serve the Master who was clearly inside this amazing sexy mass of something.

Aleshia went to wipe it away when Charlian grabbed her arm and pulled her close.

"What are you doing?" Charlian asked.

Aleshia just wanted... the mountain to kill him.
"I am serving the Master!"

Charlian just shook his head. "There is no master!"

"There is!"

"No. There. Is. Not,"

The solid mass of something became engulfed in flames. Charlian didn't even react.

"You see the flames!" Aleshia shouted.

Charlian pushed her away and started laughing.

"Babe there are no flames. There is nothing here but your delusions,"

Aleshia frowned. She hated the sound of his laughter. He was just weak, pathetic and an embarrassment.

"Kill him please!" Aleshia shouted.

But nothing happened. Aleshia took a deep breath of the wonderfully warm air and she knew, just knew that Mount Flame was correct. It wasn't time for her husband to die, he was going to die when the mountain was ready and not her.

For she was only Mount Flame's obedient servant.

Aleshia went back over to the solid mass and started to brush the thick layer of ash away. She wasn't sure what it revealed because the surface underneath was nothing more than volcanic rock.

Aleshia was at least expecting it to be glassy or something, or even see through so she could see her Master.

Then she got the urge to water the rock with blood. She looked at her husband who was standing behind her with a concerned look in his eyes, and now she understood why the glorious Mount Flame hadn't killed him.

The mountain needed him.

Aleshia looked around for a weapon or something sharp to cut him with but she couldn't see anything. Then she heard something break and she found a large shard of rock in her hand.

She didn't know how the mountain put that in her hands but clearly the mountain wanted her to use it.

Aleshia pointed it at her husband.

"Give me your hand," Aleshia said firmly.

Charlian simply stood there shaking his head. He was really that pathetic. "This isn't you,"

Aleshia chuckled and walked towards Charlian. Even now he didn't move.

"I love you Aleshia. Wake up. This isn't you,"

If she had known how strange and weird he was when Aleshia married him, she would have stopped the wedding immediately. Ever since she had been a little girl, Aleshia had wanted to be married to a rich man with power, money and someone who could give her more pleasure than she could ever wish for.

Until now and the shard of rock that started to send more and more pleasure into her mind, Aleshia hadn't realised how much time she had wasted on this low life man she called a husband.

He wasn't even worthy of that honour.

When Aleshia went over to him and stopped, she gripped his hand tight and he didn't even try to stop her. Aleshia was about to slice into his beautifully flammable flesh when she stopped.

She felt as if there was something pulling her away from the deed. For a moment she really didn't want to do this, Aleshia knew this was flat out wrong and an immense wave of pleasure came from the rock and she knew, just knew this was the right thing.

Aleshia sliced into Charlian's hand, he hissed and muttered something and then she made sure to get as much blood as possible onto the rock shard.

And to her amazement all the blood was instantly absorbed into the shard of rock.

For a moment Aleshia wondered if this would alert Charlian's stupid dragon to something being wrong, but even if that was the case there was nothing that dumb dragon could do. The glorious Mount Flame would easily defeat that useless lump of scales.

Aleshia kicked Charlian to the floor and she grinned as she watched the solid mass of volcanic rock turn blood red before turning to ash and crumbling away.

Revealing the most beautiful man she had ever seen.

The first ever man to ride a dragon was there.

Her master was lying there.

Ready to be awoken once again.

CHAPTER 12

Charlian flat out hated Mount Flame.

Even if annihilating Mount Flame was the last thing he did, Charlian was going to wipe the mountain, its corruption and whatever foul creature in front of him from the face of the Realm, and any damn maps that dared to even hint that Mount Flame had once been here.

As Charlian stared at the utterly disgusting corpse covered in ash and his strange wife Aleshia who was smiling at it, Charlian couldn't understand who this person was. That was a lie. Charlian knew exactly who it could be, but that was impossible.

Charlian focused on the male corpse's smooth skin, thick golden armour and the massive red sword that he held across his chest.

If being a professor (even a fake honourary one) had taught him anything, it was that this corpse was dressed identical to all the myths, legends and rumours surrounding the first ever human to ride a dragon.

Charlian couldn't understand how the man had been preserved for tens of thousands of years so perfectly, he had heard of magic, immortality and powerful artefacts in his military days, but surely none where powerful enough to keep this man alive for that extreme period of time?

Unless it wasn't magic that kept him alive.

Charlian really, really wanted his beautiful dragon Octon to hurry up and help him. He didn't even know if she was still alive, the bastard Mount Flame could have murdered her.

That idea scared Charlian a lot!

Then Charlian looked around at the perfectly formed cave around them that was made from volcanic rock. And it all made sense.

Charlian knew that none of the mountains in the range around Mount Flame were made from volcanic eruptions, they were all made through the smashing together of rock, sand and tectonic plates over millions of years. Volcanic rock should have been impossible.

But there was one explanation that made perfect sense to Charlian.

He couldn't even begin to amount the rage pumping through the dragon's system, but the myths always say the first dragon rider's dragon roared and unleashed torrents of flames into the mountain, to make sure the man could never live again.

What if the dragon had been horrifically wrong?

What if the dragon had killed itself trying to melt the corpse, rock and the mountain in some failed effort to make the man from living again?

Charlian nodded as he realised that the dragon had made the volcanic rock and killed itself in the process.

A tiny part of Charlian wanted them to be able to resurrect the dead dragon in some pointless attempt to help him, because surely if the man's corpse survived then maybe the dragon's corpse could too?

But Charlian doubted it. He was alone with a scary corpse, his corrupted wife and with no backup.

Aleshia's body made a hissing sound and when Charlian looked at her, he gasped as he watched his wife change.

Her hair grew longer, blacker and her eyes became bloodshot and filled with immense evil. Now Charlian knew for sure that his wife was gone.

"Beautiful, isn't he?" Aleshia said in a strange voice that wasn't her own.

"Who are you?" Charlian asked.

Aleshia tutted. "You humans are just as stupid as always. I thought you might actually grow more intelligent in ten thousand years, but you're just the same,"

For some reason Charlian recognised who was speaking, it definitely wasn't his wife, he could always, always recognise her words. But this person inside Aleshia wasn't unfamiliar, it was like… like Charlian had been learning about the speaker for decades.

"First Dragon Rider?" Charlian asked.

Aleshia turned to face him and smiled. "It wasn't that hard to figure it out. Maybe you aren't so stupid after all,"

Charlian cocked his head. This was beyond strange. "If you're in my wife, then who's the corpse,"

Aleshia hit her palm against her forehead. "Seriously!"

Charlian shrugged. He really hoped all he needed to do was try to buy Octon as much time as possible for her to save them, but Charlian doubted anything could be done now.

But if he was going to die then he had to find out everything he could first.

"Come on now human, your wife's mind was fun at first. It was open, playful and so, so curious. It was easy to influence her,"

Charlian felt his stomach tighten into an extremely painful knot.

"Your wife was as pathetic as they come. She looked into Mount Flame one day and I quietly asked for her permission to enter her mind. She never resisted, not even for a second,"

Charlian shook his head. "When was this?"

Aleshia smiled and her entire face twisted and popped and broke with the growing smile.

"Stop that!" Charlian shouted, as cold fearful sweat rolled down his back and forehead.

"Humans," Aleshia said, "you never could appreciate the world. I have been influencing and fuelling your wife's obsession for decades,"

Charlian nodded. This was perfect, it was starting to make perfect sense. It was obvious that his wife had been corrupted for ages and her obsession with the place had never made any sense until now.

There was so many questions Charlian wanted to ask, but it was clear that his corpse wanted to be resurrected and walk free again. Charlian had to stop that. He just didn't know how.

+Return to me!+ Charlian shouted inside his mind, hoping Octon would hear him and come running.

Aleshia started laughing. "Dragons. I do love killing them. Especially when their bodies drop out the sky and splash onto the ground. It's like popping a balloon,"

Charlian forced himself not to dart forward and kill the corpse and Aleshia. He had to try to keep her alive now he knew she wasn't crazy or doing this willingly.

"Why now?" Charlian asked.

Aleshia charged.

Her hands grabbed him.

Wrapping round his throat.

"Let me show you!" Aleshia shouted.

Ice grew over his body.

And Charlian's world went black.

CHAPTER 13

As soon as Aleshia woke up she instantly hated this place. She hated Mount Flame. She hated every single damn fucking thing about this place!

Aleshia looked around and hated how everything was bright white like she was floating in the clouds. She had read some silly books about magical prisons before and now she was in one, she wanted to burn down the mountain.

This was absolutely ridiculous and now she realised what had been going on for decades. Aleshia wasn't obsessed with the mountain, Mount Flame and that stupid Master.

Mount Flame had been using her!

Well that was going to end now, somehow Aleshia was going to break out of here and she was going to make the mountain know how much she hated it. She would happily bring it all crashing down.

The smell of earthy aftershave started to fill the air and it reminded Aleshia of her sexy beautiful husband that she had basically abandoned. Aleshia didn't know why she didn't resist more, she always knew deep, deep down what was happening and she let it happen anyway.

When Aleshia blinked Charlian appeared. Even now with rage filling her, Aleshia still smiled at her husband, he was so beautiful, so precious, so amazing.

He was far from pathetic, weak and whatever else that silly Master had told her to say. But Aleshia had to fix this, she had to help Charlian stop this monster.

Aleshia went over to her husband and kissed him hard. "I'm sorry. I'm-"

"I forgive you," he said softly.

Then another version of Aleshia appeared next to them. Aleshia hated what this corpse had done to her, she hated her eyes, stupidly long hair and even the black colour in it was simply awful.

The Corpse (as Aleshia was calling it) waved its hands around and the bright white dimmed to show the perfectly smooth coned-shape Mount Flame.

"Look how beautiful it is," the Corpse said. "Look how it covers the land so perfectly and look at your precious Realm,"

Then the atmosphere around them transformed, morphed and hummed to reveal a massive 3D map of the Realm with all its massive regions. From the forest-covered central regions to the snowy north and desert covered south.

"If I had known all those tribes would fall to one

another to become this Realm, I never would have gone to sleep,"

Aleshia gasped. This changed everything, the history books said he had died, but he had slept. But that actually made a lot more sense, and it explained why the corpse back in the cave looked so well preserved, because of course living things don't decay.

"Yes little humans. I never died. I never lost my power over creatures. I never stopped doing anything," the Corpse said.

Aleshia shook her head. This had to be wrong.

"Why now?" Charlian asked.

Aleshia was impressed that he could function properly, her mind was spinning out of control. Then Aleshia realised that they were trapped in her mind, her body, her soul.

All she had to do was stop the prison and somehow shut down her mind so the trap would stop. She just didn't know how.

Aleshia took deep calming breaths and simply started to let her mind drift.

"Why now?" Charlian asked again.

"You see humans, your Realm is at a turning point," the Corpse said.

Aleshia forced herself not to think, she had to let her mind go quiet.

"Your King is falling. He has as many enemies as possible. Your Realm is fighting wars in the north against the Orks, they fight in the south to stop those creatures invading,"

Charlian didn't look impressed. Aleshia closed her eyes.

"You see humans, your Realm is weakening. Even your King's children are walking to their deaths. The gay son fights so he is allowed back into the Royal Family when the Old Religion is dead. The Daughter walks into a conspiracy she cannot even start to understand,"

Aleshia forced herself not to even entertain any of those ideas. She simply had to… all noise disappeared from her mind and immense pleasure replaced it as Aleshia went completely mindless.

She opened her eyes and even more pleasure filled her, and Aleshia started to realise that the Corpse was using his moment to attack and return because the Realm was arguably at its weakest.

She knew about the wars in the North, South and the troubles with the dwarfs and elves in the East and West. Trouble surrounded the entire Realm and a massive attack from within would threaten to rip the Realm apart.

Millions would die, and Aleshia couldn't allow that to happen.

Aleshia screamed as loud as she could. Rage built within her. She wanted to kill. She wanted to lash out.

Cracks appeared in her mind.

Blinking light attacked her.

It melted her eyes.

Aleshia kept screaming.

The light kept attacking her.

Aleshia heard her husband. He was screaming with her.

More and more cracks appeared.

Aleshia and Charlian screamed as one.

The prison shattered.

They were free.

CHAPTER 14

Charlian was going to slaughter the Corpse!

The disgusting ice melted away as Charlian smashed open his eyes and he sprung into action.

The volcanic cave shook. Charlian looked at Aleshia, her eyes were opening.

But when they both looked at the disgusting corpse of the first dragon rider, he was moving, his arms were grabbing his sword. Raising it into the air.

Aleshia grabbed a shard of rock.

Charging at the Corpse.

Thrusting it into his chest.

The Corpse went limp.

Charlian slowly started to walk over to the disgraceful corpse and it certainly looked dead, but it had before when it had possessed Aleshia.

The Corpse jumped up.

Swinging his sword.

Charlian pushed Aleshia away.

The sword sliced his arm.

Charlian hissed.

The Corpse flew forward.

Waving the sword.

He was alive.

Charlian rolled back.

Again and again.

Aleshia jumped into the air.

Tackling the Corpse.

She whacked him.

Charlian jumped him.

The Corpse shrieked.

Aleshia screamed in agony.

Her ears bleed.

The Corpse smashed his fists into her.

Charlian charged over.

The Corpse waved his hands.

Both Charlian and Aleshia froze instantly and Charlian was really, really starting to wish he had kept his military sword instead of returning it when he left.

If he had the sword, Charlian could easily slice through this witch abomination and save his wife.

The Corpse went over to Charlian and sliced his face. It burned and Charlian felt crippling pain fill him. It felt like his face was fire!

"Stop!" Aleshia screamed.

The Corpse shook his head. "I need strength my love. I am returned but weak. This is only a fraction of my power,"

Charlian watched as the Corpse looked him in the eye and started to borrow into his soul.

Charlian screamed as the Corpse drained the life out of him. He felt weaker and weaker by the second.

The entire cave shook violently. The Corpse stopped.

Charlian took massive deep breaths as he tried to regain his energy. He had to stop this Corpse and kill him.

The Corpse flicked his wrists and both Charlian and Aleshia fell hard onto the rough cave floor.

As much as Charlian wanted to jump up and wrap his hands around the Corpse's throat, he knew that was completely useless. He had to think of something else.

Aleshia hissed.

She jumped up.

Flying at him.

She leapt into the air.

Kicking him in the head.

The Corpse smashed onto the ground.

Charlian flew forward.

Grabbing his head.

Smashing it onto the ground.

Blood spattered out.

The Corpse whistled and as he whistled a merry little tune to himself, Charlian felt like he had lost complete control over his hands as his own hands moved, and wrapped themselves loving around his own throat.

Charlian wanted to let go and kill the Corpse, but his hands would never obey him. Even Aleshia was doing the same, Charlian was really starting to get pissed off at the Corpse.

"You two are interesting, I'll give you that. I will miss you both when you die. Not," the Corpse said.

The Corpse started whistling again and Charlian's hands started to squeeze and Charlian gagged.

The cave shook again and again.

Chunks of rock smashed down.

Charlian's hands squeezed hard.

And harder.

And harder.

Charlian forced his mind to focus. He was not dying here. His hands started to obey.

The whistling got louder.

The cave shook again.

It felt like an earthquake.

Something exploded.

Something massive was thundering towards them.

"Fuck off from my boss!" Octon shouted.

The Corpse shot out his hand.

Octon flew at him.

She roared as loud as she could

Charlian's hands let go.

Aleshia and Charlian charged together.

Octon flew past them.

Charlian and Aleshia leapt into the air.

All three of them zoomed towards the Corpse.

He tried to run.

Octon roared.

Unleashing a torrent of black fire.

The Corpse screamed.

The fire smashed into him.

Charlian and Aleshia smashed their fists into his skull.

Shattering him.

As they both watched as Octon's terrifying black fire engulf the Corpse and turn it to atoms, Charlian felt a massive wave of relief wash over him.

And all Charlian wanted in that moment was to kiss, snog and love the amazing wife that he had loved for decades and he finally had her back.

Charlian went over to her, and pressed his lips hard against her.

CHAPTER 15

As Charlian felt the wonderful hard saddle of Octon under him as him, Octon and Aleshia flew through the freezing cold air back towards their base, Charlian just stared out over the frozen wastelands.

Charlian held Aleshia tightly in his arms, loving the feeling of her wonderfully soft hair against his chin and the warm feeling of her against him.

After everything that had happened in the past two days, Charlian wasn't sure what was going to happen now, in a way their entire life had changed, because now he actually had his wife back.

The air smelt awfully cold, but now Charlian was really starting to get used to it, and maybe the frozen wastelands weren't such a bad thing after all. Maybe he could spend a little time while up here in the mountains, he could try skiing, snowboarding or even fly with Octon into the middle of a blizzard like she wanted.

That would be fun!

The howl of the wind gently passed them as the three of them soared through the sky, and Charlian realised there really was nothing like flying on an amazing dragon and with a beautiful woman in his arms.

Maybe things had changed a lot in the past two days but the only thing that hadn't changed for Charlian, was how much he loved both the stunning women in his life. He was going to keep exploring, loving and protecting Aleshia and Octon for a long, long time.

As Octon banked a little in the sky, Charlian held Aleshia tighter and he realised that he had actually missed this. Charlian loved the feeling of pure power and chemistry between them, and Charlian hadn't realised that had been missing for a long time.

In a way Charlian supposed that the two of them would be like entering a new relationship, it sounded as strange as learning that a corpse had been sleeping and not dead for tens of thousands of years, but now Charlian knew that he had to get to know Aleshia again now she wasn't possessed.

A lot of men might have just given up, dumped Aleshia off in the nearest village, town or city, but Charlian was never going to do that. He wanted her, he wanted to love her forever.

Of course there were going to be challenges ahead, and he might even have to help Aleshia discover who she was again, but he looked forward to it. Because he truly believed in all the vows he took when he married her.

Through war, sickness and plague, Charlian was going to be by her side and helping with whatever she needed. He was that sort of man.

Charlian kissed the back of Aleshia's warm neck as he just wondered about how lucky he was. If it was any other situation or if he had been back in the military, Charlian probably would have to have killed Aleshia for being a threat.

He was more than glad it hadn't come to that.

But what made it worse was Charlian knew he would have killed her. It might have been decades of military conditioning, service or dedication to the King, but Charlian just knew if he had to, he would have ended the love of his life.

Of course Aleshia would have understood and if he was the corrupted one, she would have done the same, but Charlian still felt guilty about it. He just wished he didn't have that sort of courage.

Then he reminded himself that everyone had ended up okay. His wife was alive, and that was all that mattered.

And Charlian would never be able to repay Octon for the amazing thing she had done for him. She had saved them when they were all certain that the Realm was doomed and Charlian was going to die.

Octon was always amazing, loveable and furious at the enemy. That was actually why he had picked her as a Dragonlet when others had rejected her.

Charlian was glad he had chosen so well.

When the three of them had been packing up, Charlian had questioned her about how she had known they were in danger. Apparently she hadn't heard him sending his thoughts to her.

There was something a lot cooler so she said.

All Dragon Riders (which Charlian was) and dragons had to bond before they entered service, Charlian thought that meant like friends at first, then he found out it meant spiritually so their very souls were connected.

When Charlian was in danger, his fear, rage and love rippled throughout the magic realm and slammed into Octon's soul, so she knew exactly where he was and what was happening.

So she flew. And by God-King did she fly.

Charlian was extremely grateful for that, and he was definitely going to take her for that fly in the blizzard.

Yet there was one thing Charlian could never shake, he wasn't sure he wanted to do this… expeditionary stuff anymore for the university and that pompous idiot Durcan.

There were other amazing ways to explore, the two of them could be contractors, join the military or simply explore the world on their own terms. They were both rich enough and Charlian's pay off when he left the military was large enough so the world was truly their oyster.

That idea made Charlian smile, they really could do that, they really could just explore the history of the world and learn about it in their own way.

No more university politics, budgets and hierarchies. Charlian would even be able to get away from the fighting and horrible arguing when he took a legendary finding to the university press, and they apparently couldn't publish it because he wasn't a real professor.

Charlian felt his excitement build and build and build at that realisation, he could teach history to the masses without the university.

When Octon started to slow down, Charlian smiled as he saw the small log cabins on the ground and everyone running out to meet them. He didn't know why they were so excited, but they were.

And Charlian realised that he was excited too.

Not because he was returning to them. But because he was here, alive and well, with the two most precious women in his life.

And Charlian loved that.

CHAPTER 16

Professor Aleshia sat on her cold, hard rocking chair looking out over the mountain range and Mount Flame and all its wonderfully picturesque blanket of snow, she just wasn't sure she liked it here anymore.

Aleshia picked up her massive mug of steaming coffee with some spices floating around it in, and she couldn't shake the feeling that she just wasn't happy here anymore.

Was she ever truly happy here?

Aleshia hated herself for everything that had happened. She had been influenced, corrupted and used for decades by that first dragon rider who wanted to raise up and kill everyone. Aleshia didn't think she could ever forgive herself for that.

If anyone ever asked why she had been corrupted, Aleshia knew the exact answer she would have told them. She had been so focused on proving herself better than her siblings and parents that she had been willing to sell her soul to the demons to do it.

And in a strange twisted way, Aleshia supposed she had. Aleshia hadn't tried to resist the corrupting voice in the back of her mind, she always knew it had been there but she never paid it much attention.

In all honesty, Aleshia believed it was helping her. But helping her do what? Be silly, arrogant and almost kill her husband?

That was probably the truth and Aleshia just wished, just wished with all her heart that she could go back to the past and change it.

The sound of people laughing, talking and joking around actually made Aleshia smile, it used to annoy the corrupting voice in her head, but it really did delight Aleshia. It meant her people, her amazing people were happy and that was what Aleshia's life was all about.

It wasn't about proving herself, she knew that she wasn't, but she could at least try to improve lives and make a few people laugh along the way. Because that's what history was truly about, history gave people a chance to escape their everyday life for a few hours and explore another world, it meant they could laugh, joke or even be horrified about how people used to live.

That's why she studied Pre-Real history and that was why she was always going to do it, no matter what.

The sound of the cabin's door opening and closing made Aleshia's stomach tighten as she knew it was her beautiful sexy husband. Aleshia turned to face him and he was smiling at her.

She didn't understand why he wasn't angry, rageful or disappointed at her, but she supposed that was why she loved him. He really was that rare type of husband that always supported, worshipped and just loved her no matter what.

Aleshia knew exactly how lucky she was to have a man like that, she knew plenty of men who would have killed her back in that cave. In truth she knew he would have.

And she was surprisingly okay with that, because she had always known she had married a soldier. A man who was sworn to protect the Realm, its citizens and its land from enemies, and Aleshia loved that about him.

To her it meant he was protecting the culture and she wanted to continue for as long as possible, because the longer a culture lasts for, the more interesting things that can happen for future historians to study.

Maybe someone might study her and her work one day. She doubted it but it would be nice.

Charlian walked over to Aleshia and he took her hands, pulled her up and kissed her. Aleshia wrapped her arms around him and just felt the chemistry, love and affection flow between them.

He kissed her.

"What happens now?" Aleshia asked, fearing he would leave her.

Charlian frowned. "I can't go back to the University. I hate it. I just want you,"

Aleshia kissed him again and hugged him tight. Before he said that she had been wondering about going back to the university, having to answer Durcan's pointless questions and just... the repetitiveness of it all. Go on an expedition, answer lots of bureaucracy and then publish an academic paper.

Aleshia loved the exploring and writing of her papers. It was just the questions and snobbish academics she hated.

"Let's never go back there," Aleshia said smiling.

Charlian's face lit up. "Thanks. There's an entire Realm to explore,"

Aleshia felt her face turn bright red and her stomach started to do little flips of excitement. Now that damn corrupting voice wasn't in her mind, her mind was thinking about all the other amazing cultures and ruins and possibilities in the Realm.

And beyond!

Aleshia pushed away from her husband and looked at all her amazing history books on the floor and covering the bed. There were so many tens of thousands of years of history to explore.

Aleshia and Charlian just looked at each other.

"There's a lot of history to explore. There's a lot of cultures to discover," Aleshia said with a massive smile.

"You're truly back aren't you?"

Aleshia felt so young as her energy returned and she just wanted to run off into the wilderness of the Realm and discover all of its secrets.

"I'm definitely back!" Aleshia shouted with happiness. "Now let's find us some history!"

As Aleshia and Charlian grabbed hands and ran over to their history books to start planning their next move, Aleshia realised this was all she had ever wanted.

And it had only taken a strange supernatural possession to make her see, all she had ever wanted to explore the Realm with a sexy, beautiful man.

And that's what she was going to do. She was going to explore the Realm from one edge to another then another with the amazing man she loved, and she was really, really looking forward to that.

GET YOUR FREE AND EXCLUSIVE SHORT STORY NOW! LEARN ABOUT NEMESIO'S PAST!

https://www.subscribepage.com/fireheart

Keep up to date with exclusive deals on Connor Whiteley's Books, as well as the latest news about new releases and so much more!

Sign up for the Grab a Book and Chill Monthly newsletter, and you'll get one **FREE** ebook just for signing up: Agents of The Emperor Collection.

Sign Up Now!

https://dl.bookfunnel.com/f4p5xkprbk

About the author:

Connor Whiteley is the author of over 60 books in the sci-fi fantasy, nonfiction psychology and books for writer's genre and he is a Human Branding Speaker and Consultant.

He is a passionate warhammer 40,000 reader, psychology student and author.

Who narrates his own audiobooks and he hosts The Psychology World Podcast.

All whilst studying Psychology at the University of Kent, England.

Also, he was a former Explorer Scout where he gave a speech to the Maltese President in August 2018 and he attended Prince Charles' 70th Birthday Party at Buckingham Palace in May 2018.

Plus, he is a self-confessed coffee lover!

OTHER SHORT STORIES BY CONNOR WHITELEY

Blade of The Emperor
Arbiter's Truth
The Bloodied Rose
Asmodia's Wrath
Heart of A Killer
Emissary of Blood
Computation of Battle
Old One's Wrath
Puppets and Masters
Ship of Plague
Interrogation
Edge of Failure
One Way Choice
Acceptable Losses
Balance of Power
Good Idea At The Time
Escape Plan
Escape In The Hesitation
Inspiration In Need
Singing Warriors
Dragon Coins
Dragon Tea
Dragon Rider
Knowledge is Power
Killer of Polluters
Climate of Death
Sacrifice of the Soul
Heart of The Flesheater

Heart of The Regent
Heart of The Standing
Feline of The Lost
Heart of The Story
The Family Mailing Affair
Defining Criminality
The Martian Affair
A Cheating Affair
The Little Café Affair
Mountain of Death
Prisoner's Fight
Claws of Death
Bitter Air
Honey Hunt
Blade On A Train
City of Fire
Awaiting Death
Poison In The Candy Cane
Christmas Innocence
You Better Watch Out
Christmas Theft
Trouble In Christmas
Smell of The Lake
Problem In A Car
Theft, Past and Team
Embezzler In The Room
A Strange Way To Go
A Horrible Way To Go
Ann Awful Way To Go
An Old Way To Go

A Fishy Way To Go
A Pointy Way To Go
A High Way To Go
A Fiery Way To Go
A Glassy Way To Go
A Chocolatey Way To Go
Kendra Detective Mystery Collection Volume 1
Kendra Detective Mystery Collection Volume 2
Stealing A Chance At Freedom
Glassblowing and Death
Theft of Independence
Cookie Thief
Marble Thief
Book Thief
Art Thief

Other books by Connor Whiteley:

The Fireheart Fantasy Series
Heart of Fire
Heart of Lies
Heart of Prophecy
Heart of Bones
Heart of Fate

City of Assassins (Urban Fantasy)
City of Death
City of Marytrs
City of Pleasure
City of Power

Agents of The Emperor
Return of The Ancient Ones
Vigilance
Angels of Fire

The Garro Series- Fantasy/Sci-fi
GARRO: GALAXY'S END
GARRO: RISE OF THE ORDER
GARRO: END TIMES
GARRO: SHORT STORIES
GARRO: COLLECTION
GARRO: HERESY
GARRO: FAITHLESS
GARRO: DESTROYER OF WORLDS
GARRO: COLLECTIONS BOOK 4-6

GARRO: MISTRESS OF BLOOD
GARRO: BEACON OF HOPE
GARRO: END OF DAYS

Winter Series- Fantasy Trilogy Books
WINTER'S COMING
WINTER'S HUNT
WINTER'S REVENGE
WINTER'S DISSENSION

Bettie English Private Eye Series
A Very Private Woman
The Russian Case

Miscellaneous:
RETURN
FREEDOM
SALVATION
Reflection of Mount Flame
The Masked One
The Great Deer

All books in 'An Introductory Series':

BIOLOGICAL PSYCHOLOGY 3RD EDITION
COGNITIVE PSYCHOLOGY THIRD EDITION
SOCIAL PSYCHOLOGY- 3RD EDITION
ABNORMAL PSYCHOLOGY 3RD EDITION
PSYCHOLOGY OF RELATIONSHIPS- 3RD EDITION
DEVELOPMENTAL PSYCHOLOGY 3RD EDITION
HEALTH PSYCHOLOGY
RESEARCH IN PSYCHOLOGY
A GUIDE TO MENTAL HEALTH AND TREATMENT AROUND THE WORLD- A GLOBAL LOOK AT DEPRESSION
FORENSIC PSYCHOLOGY
THE FORENSIC PSYCHOLOGY OF THEFT, BURGLARY AND OTHER CRIMES AGAINST PROPERTY
CRIMINAL PROFILING: A FORENSIC PSYCHOLOGY GUIDE TO FBI PROFILING AND GEOGRAPHICAL AND STATISTICAL PROFILING.
CLINICAL PSYCHOLOGY
FORMULATION IN PSYCHOTHERAPY
PERSONALITY PSYCHOLOGY AND INDIVIDUAL DIFFERENCES
CLINICAL PSYCHOLOGY REFLECTIONS VOLUME 1
CLINICAL PSYCHOLOGY REFLECTIONS VOLUME 2

CULT PSYCHOLOGY
Police Psychology

www.ingramcontent.com/pod-product-compliance
Lightning Source LLC
LaVergne TN
LVHW011848060526
838200LV00054B/4220